VISIT AMAZON.COM FOR MORE
LITTLE HEDGEHOG BOOKS

MY PAPPY
LOVES ME

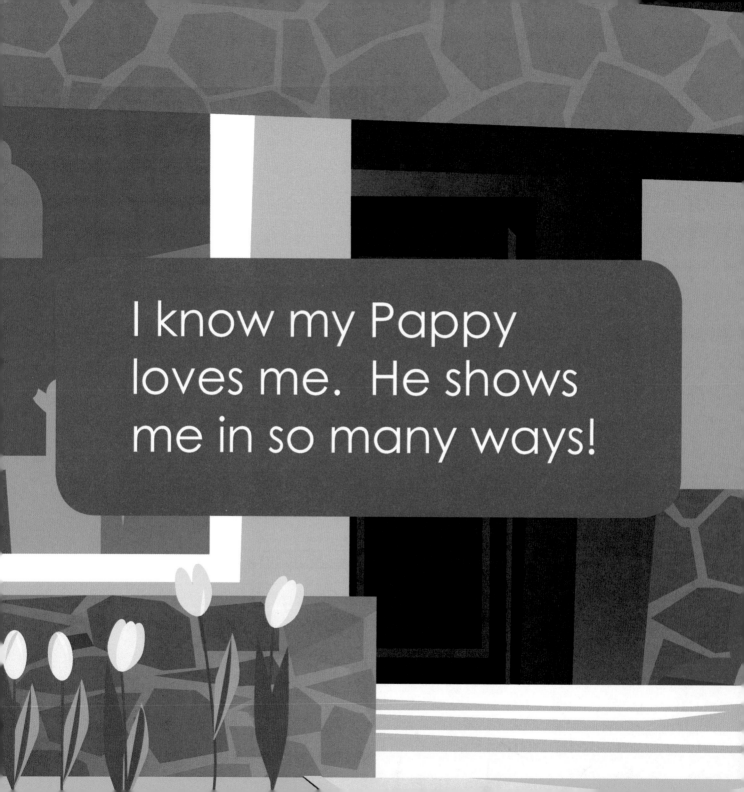

I know my Pappy loves me. He shows me in so many ways!

When I spend the night, he reads me a book at bedtime.

Pappy lets me help him with his garden.

Sometimes, Pappy picks me up from school. He's always excited to see me!

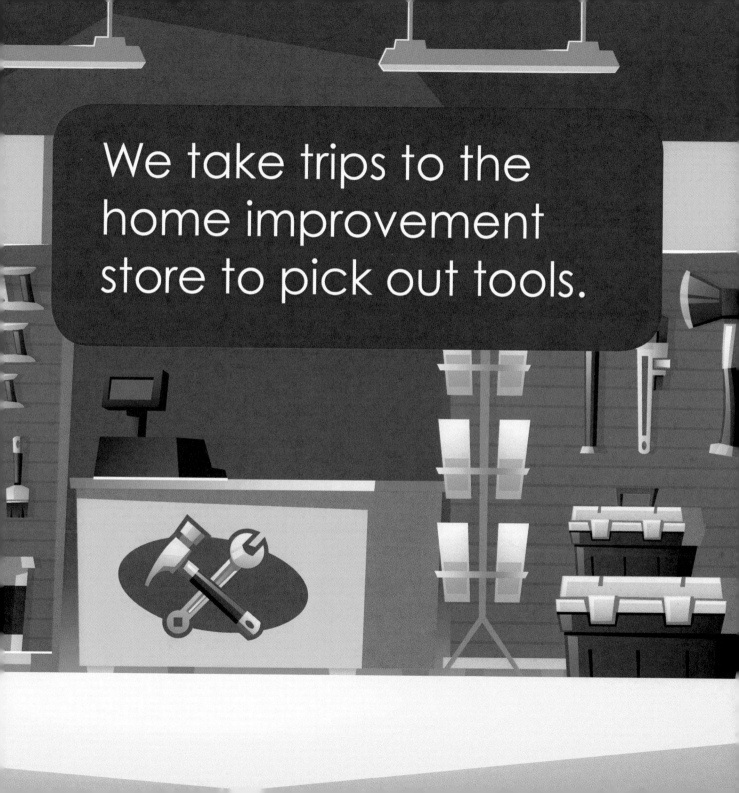

We take trips to the home improvement store to pick out tools.

When it is autumn, we take walks through the neighborhood to see the pretty leaves.

In winter, we still go on fun adventures. Even if it's cold out!

At Christmastime, we look at the twinkling lights together.

Made in the USA
Middletown, DE
23 May 2023

31287872R00020